THE MISSIN OF LAUGHTER

For long years there has been an important gap in our knowledge of the development of the comic theater from the politically and intellectually oriented comedies of Aristophanes to the plot of the thwarted lovers and the domestic comedies of later eras. We have known that the key figure of this major transition was the Greek dramatist Menander, but until recently we have had only a pale conception of his contribution.

With the discovery and translation of *The Dyskolos* ("The Grouch"), Menander at last comes alive for us, with his world of troubled lovers, scheming servants, foolish old men, witty dialogue, and quick turnabouts in plot. In this play about an outrageous misanthrope, the mischief he causes, and the comeuppance he receives, we encounter a comic spirit that Molière would have bowed to in homage, and that we can freshly enjoy today.

ABOUT THE TRANSLATOR: CARROLL MOULTON was educated as a classical scholar at Harvard and Yale. He currently teaches classics at Princeton University.

THE
DYSKOLOS

by

MENANDER

TRANSLATED
WITH AN INTRODUCTION
AND NOTES BY

Carroll Moulton

A MERIDIAN CLASSIC
NEW AMERICAN LIBRARY

NEW YORK AND SCARBOROUGH, ONTARIO

NAL BOOKS ARE AVAILABLE AT QUANTITY DISCOUNTS
WHEN USED TO PROMOTE PRODUCTS OR SERVICES. FOR
INFORMATION PLEASE WRITE TO PREMIUM MARKETING
DIVISION, NEW AMERICAN LIBRARY, 1633 BROADWAY,
NEW YORK, NEW YORK 10019.

Copyright © 1977 by Carroll Moulton

Library of Congress Catalog Card Number: 84-60053

MERIDIAN CLASSIC TRADEMARK REG. U.S. PAT. OFF. AND FOREIGN COUNTRIES
REGISTERED TRADEMARK—MARCA REGISTRADA
HECHO EN WINNIPEG, CANADA

SIGNET, SIGNET CLASSIC, MENTOR, PLUME, MERIDIAN AND NAL BOOKS
are published in the United States by
New American Library,
1633 Broadway, New York, New York 10019,
in Canada by New American Library of Canada Limited,
81 Mack Avenue, Scarborough, Ontario, M1L 1M8

First Meridian Classic Printing, 1984

2   3   4   5   6   7   8   9

PRINTED IN CANADA

For Erich and Karen

CONTENTS

PREFACE

MENANDER'S *Dyskolos (The Grouch)* was first published in 1959; there have been several English translations since that date. I undertook a new rendering essentially for three reasons. First, to my knowledge, there is no readily available American verse translation, and this seems to me a serious lack. One is constantly reminded that diction and the rhythms of speech differ on both sides of the Atlantic, although the language is officially the same. The differences are especially important in comic drama, which so frequently employs colloquial speech. Furthermore, Menander wrote in verse, a verse so limpid, to be sure, that it approaches the rhythms of prose. But in antiquity, he was celebrated as a poet. Prose translations of his one complete surviving play have always seemed to me to sacrifice an important formal characteristic of the original, whatever they have gained in immediacy of appeal.

Secondly, recent work on Menander's style has painstakingly proved what common sense might have suggested all along: Menander's Greek is indeed elegant and homogeneous (certainly when compared, say, to the wide variations in style in any comedy of Aristophanes); but it is also supple enough to be adjusted delicately to characterization and dramatic purpose. In other words, within a rather narrow spectrum, Menander manipulates diction for the individual portrayal of character. The subtlety of this process may be judged by consulting the article of F. H. Sandbach, "Menander's Manipulation of Language for Dramatic Purposes," published in 1970 and included in the bibliography at the end of this volume. Our more sophisticated understanding of Menander's style

seemed to me to warrant a new translation of the *Dyskolos,*
and in what follows I have especially tried to take account of
how the style of the original bears on characterization.

Finally, the appearance in 1972 of Sandbach's Oxford text
of the plays and principal fragments of Menander was an important landmark in scholarship. Since much of the material
has come to light within the last fifteen years, the effort to
make it accessible naturally involved widely scattered publication. And since the reading of tattered papyri is a difficult
and often controversial project for highly trained scholars,
there has been a fair amount of disagreement on what
Menander actually wrote at many places in the text. The
appearance of Sandbach's edition means that, for the first
time, all of Menander's dramatic output is collected in one
place. Furthermore, his critical apparatus on the text gathers
together the often valuable alternative conjectures by other
scholars. This is likely, then, to be the standard edition of
Menander for some time. In 1973, Sandbach published a
commentary compiled by him and the late A. W. Gomme (see
bibliography). Like his text, the commentary provides us, on
questions of literary interpretation, with distinguished scholarly
criticism, together with a summary of the principal work
published up to 1973. It, too, is very likely to prove a standard
work.

The appearance of these two major works of scholarship, if
nothing else, would justify a new translation of the *Dyskolos.*
No other version in English has been able to take account of
the considerable progress in Menandrian studies that they
represent. In this translation, I have followed, almost without
exception, Sandbach's text, and I have been greatly aided by
his commentary. I have profited much, too, from the edition
and commentary of E. W. Handley, which remains one of
the finest works on the *Dyskolos.*

For suggestions and encouragement, it is a pleasure to
acknowledge the help of my family, of S. D. Atkins, F. C.
Bourne, W. R. Colson, H. Lloyd-Jones, the Mantell family,
and especially of C. Boyd. One more debt remains to be re-
corded. As a graduate student, I was first afforded an op-

portunity to lecture at Yale University by Erich Segal: that lecture happened to be on the *Dyskolos*. Our talks on ancient comedy and the still vital tradition that proceeds from it have taught me most of what I know on the subject. To Erich and his wife Karen, then, this effort is affectionately dedicated.

Princeton, New Jersey
1 November 1975

INTRODUCTION

I

IF Rembrandt had been known merely from sketches and descriptions, the sudden discovery of one canvas in good condition would have caused enormous excitement. This is quite what happened in the world of letters with the publication in 1959 of Menander's *Dyskolos*. It was then, and remains now, the only complete extant play of the most celebrated dramatist of the Greek "New Comedy," the genre which evolved after Aristophanes and which flourished in Athens in the late fourth and early third century B.C. To be sure, fragments of Menander already existed, including sizable portions of three other plays, discovered in 1905. But, as Aristotle says in the *Poetics* of the plot of tragedy, every play should have a beginning, a middle, and an end. And only within the last fifteen years have readers been able to appraise a Menandrian drama from start to finish.

Those years have also witnessed the release of other new fragments: most significantly, they have supplemented what we already possessed of another comedy by Menander, *The Woman of Samos*, so that we now have all but about one hundred and fifty verses of that play.

The stir created by these finds was shared not only by classical scholars but by all students of European literature for two reasons. First was the importance of Menander in literary history, as the source of the Western tradition in comedy. Long before the discovery of sizable fragments of the plays, for example, George Meredith coupled Menander with Molière: "[They] stand alone specially as comic poets of the feelings and the idea" (*An Essay on Comedy*, 1877).

The avowed debt of the Roman playwright Terence to Greek
New Comedy, and to Menander in particular, showed
Meredith that the ancient tradition proceeded from New
Comedy to the Romans, and thence to Shakespeare and
Molière. Indeed, a critic of Aristophanes, the most famous
playwright of the so-called Old Comedy in late fifth-century
Athens, was later to say that that poet died "intestate." Whatever the validity of Meredith's theory of comedy in general,
his appraisal of Menander, whom he could only know through
the filter of Plautus and Terence, was prescient: the title
character of the *Dyskolos* reminds us of no one so much
as a protagonist in Molière, consumed by an obsession, but
human *malgré lui*.

Menander was known not only as a source. The testimony
of the ancients, who still could read and attend his plays,
reckoned him high in the ranks of dramatic poets for his own
merits. Julius Caesar, who had dreams of literary glory, was
forced to admit that his favorite Terence was still only a
dimidiatus Menander, a Menander "cut down by half."
Quintilian (c. 35–100 A.D.), Rome's first professor of literary
criticism, says that the careful study of Menander alone would
suffice to make one a good orator: his splendor so far out-
shines all other writers of comedy that he has scarcely left
them a name. Quintilian's contemporary Plutarch asks rhetorically: "For what other reason, truly, would an educated
man go to the theater except to see Menander?" And roughly
one hundred years after the poet's death, Aristophanes of
Byzantium, scholar and critic in Alexandria, effusively ex-
claimed: "Oh Menander! Oh, life! Which of you imitated the
other?"

Prominent in many of these tributes is the theme of
Menander's realism, and it is to this often noticed, but ill
defined, aspect of his work that we must presently turn. First,
however, a few facts about the playwright's life and background. Born in Athens in 342 B.C., about a century after the
birth of Aristophanes, Menander produced over one hundred
plays in a working career of some thirty years (he died

c. 291 B.C.). Like Aristophanes, Menander started young: probably his first play was staged when he was twenty. Ancient sources preserve few details about his life. For whatever it is worth, he is said to have learned his craft from the older comic poet Alexis, to have been a pupil of the philosopher Theophrastus (who was, in turn, the pupil of Aristotle), and to have met death by drowning when he was swimming at the Piraeus. In fact, we know not very much more or less about his life than about any of the great Greek dramatists.

But we can specify that Menander's Athens was a very different place from the city of Sophocles, Euripides, and Aristophanes. The celebrated Athenian democracy had long since fallen, and the city was, during much of Menander's life, a garrison town under the rule of the Macedonian successors of Alexander the Great, who died when the playwright was nineteen. The political turmoil of Menander's age, unlike that of a century before, did not allow the license of satire or invective to the comic stage; though topical references may occasionally be found in Menander's plays, he, like other poets of the New Comedy (his most famous rivals were Diphilos and Philemon), preferred to confine his plots to the sphere of private life.

Those pigeonholing phrases of evolution, "Old," "Middle," and "New Comedy," arc far less definitive than is commonly assumed. Subjects, themes, and styles overlap in the hundred years that take us from Aristophanes down to Alexis and then to Menander, and no literature develops in ways that are so neatly schematic as such a tripartite division may suggest. Yet, on any measure, the contrast between the fifth-century comedies of Aristophanes and Menander's *Dyskolos* is striking. Gone is the extravagant mixture of ribaldry and lyricism, the flights of fantasy in plot, the personal and topical invective, the avowed concern with civic life. Most singularly missing, too, is that extraordinary creation, the Aristophanic hero, who follows a fantastic course of self-aggrandizement through a mixture of inspired whimsy and sophistic wheedling.

Compare the end of the *Wasps* with the end of the *Dyskolos*,
for example. Aristophanes' hero, old Philocleon, returns drunk
from a party, having stolen someone else's girl and enlivened
his progress home by beating up people in the street. Eagerly
anticipating a sexual orgy, he turns aside the protests of his
son and crowns his physical exuberance at the finale with a
wild dance. A very different party is in progress at the end
of the *Dyskolos:* a decorous, middle-class wedding feast. In
the final scene, the hints of physical aggression by Daos and
Sikon are only hints: Knemon is tamed verbally and psycho-
logically. In Menander, the Aristophanic inversion of the
generations is abandoned. The *Wasps* presents a mischievous,
carousing father who chafes under the restraint of his sober
son, and who is eager for *kōmos* (revelry) and *gamos* (sex).
In the *Dyskolos* it is the young who properly look forward to
a *gamos* (here a legitimized marriage), and the old who are
reproached for hardening of the arteries. Knemon is eventu-
ally persuaded, of course, to go to the party at the end of
the play. Although this may represent the process of social
reintegration which is often described as a function of
comedy in general, the play nevertheless leaves us with the
impression that the success of Daos and Sikon with the old
man has been strictly limited. After all, we never do see
Knemon dance.

If the sketch above testifies to some of the differences between the fifth and fourth century Athenian comic stage, it
may also indicate some of the thematic continuities. In fact,
the two finales we have been considering are structurally
similar, and it is possible that psychological criticism would
regard the second as merely a "sublimated" version of the
first. On stage, the scene from Menander, if less outrageous, is
potentially just as funny: New Comedy is more theatrically
energetic than is often supposed. Clearly, however, this energy
differs from that of Aristophanes. It has, in the main, been
elevated from satire and farce to the realms of romantic
comedy and the comedy of manners.

It may be that what we miss most vividly in Greek New

Comedy, when we compare it to Aristophanes, is a sense of variety. All that we know of Menander's plots conforms to a basic pattern, in which the union of lovers triumphs after being blocked by a series of obstacles. The scene is often the same: a street in or near Athens. And there are conventional character types: the young lovers, the household slaves, the old fathers, the parasites, the self-important cooks, the soldiers, the whores. All this makes it understandable that New Comedy plots are difficult to remember in individual detail. On the other hand, despite the brilliant theory of F. M. Cornford on the common structural elements of Old Comedy (in *The Origins of Old Attic Comedy*, 1914), who can forget the details of an Aristophanic play? Action and character, far more exaggerated than in Menander, must necessarily seem more individualized as well.

And yet this view requires some balancing. For the conventions of New Comedy not only admitted of individualization in plot and character, they required it. "Jack shall have Jill/Nought shall go ill"—but *how?* The interest for an audience, ancient or modern, lies in the particular working out of the romance. In what way will the obstacles, or blocking characters, be surmounted? The analogy of fifth-century tragedy is not inappropriate here. Everyone knew that Agamemnon would be murdered, that Oedipus would discover his terrifying past, that Herakles would go mad and slay his children. But it was the brilliance of the great Attic dramatists, at least in part, that they took well-known myths and particularized them. It is worth recalling that the predecessor most admired by the poets of the New Comedy was Euripides the tragedian, and Euripides was famous for his highly individual, and unexpected, treatments of the old stories. As to character, and the diction that reflects it, Menander is here too, for all his superficial homogeneity, an individualizing artist. The strokes are more subtle, and the limits more narrow, than in Aristophanes. A plainer recognition of them may emerge from an analysis of the *Dyskolos* itself.

II

The *Dyskolos* was produced in 317 at the Lenaian festival, and won its author first prize. It exhibits many of the themes and characters, and the basic plot, typical of New Comedy. Coincidence (*tychē*), love at first sight, and concern with the family unit and social status are all important themes. The old father (the *senex* of Roman comedy), the young lover (*adulescens*), and the cook are leading roles. The setting is Phyle, a country district near Athens, and the stage presents two houses: one is the dwelling of Knemon the *dyskolos* (or "grouch"), his daughter, and his old servant Simiche; in the other live his estranged wife, his stepson Gorgias, and their servant Daos. Between the houses is a shrine dedicated to the Nymphs and to the rural god Pan: it is this deity who speaks the prologue. All the other characters of the play arrive from the city to intrude on this suburban world.

The theme of city vs. country is indeed important in the *Dyskolos,* and is explicitly emphasized in the contrast between the appearance, attitudes, and speech of the two young men, Sostratos and Gorgias. For example, much is made of Sostratos' fancy city clothes (cf. 255ff, 363ff):

DAOS [*staring offstage*]
Hold on a bit. We haven't come in vain.
As I predicted, our man's come back.
[*Enter* SOSTRATOS]

GORGIAS
You mean that one who's wearing fancy clothes?

DAOS
That's him!

GORGIAS
A rascal, judging by his looks

* * *

DAOS [*interrupting*]
                    Hold on!
You're going to stand around in fancy clothes
while we're at work?

SOSTRATOS
Why not?

We must imagine, too, that Gorgias delivers as fine an accolade as he can when he pronounces Sostratos' wealthy father "quite a farmer" at 775. It is Kallippides who blesses the double wedding at play's end: appropriately, he unites urban and rustic virtue. But the theme of city vs. country is not only exploited in connection with the romantic plot. It appears too in the minor characterizations. Contrast, for example, the uninhibited élan of Sikon the cook and Chaireas the parasite (both from the city) with the simple-mindedness of Simiche, Knemon's maid, or with the suspicious vindictiveness of Daos, the servant of Gorgias.

And, within the "city" group of characters, there are further distinctions. Chaireas, who appears only in the first scene, is presented as a vignette of the "braggart parasite." Essential to his characterization is that he leave, and quickly, with someone else holding the bag. Hence, objections to the lack of development in his portrayal entirely miss Menander's ironic point. Sikon is another matter. Although many critics have regarded the cooks of New Comedy as one-dimensional and interchangeable, here we have a well-rounded portrait. Sikon's egomaniacal authoritarianism is set against his uniquely colorful language: he uses more metaphors, swears by more gods, and is more lyrically effusive than any other character in the play. Consider particularly his description of the party at 931ff, where eloquent enthusiasm is pungently combined with a concern for his professional reputation and with his desire to teach Knemon a lesson.

SIKON [*sternly*]
Sit still, and don't you grumble!
You're antisocial. You hate women. You won't come
to where we sacrifice. You'll have to bear all this, then.
There's no one here to help you. Go on and bite your
tongue . . .
. . . Your wife and daughter first were welcomed with a
kiss,

and now they're having a most pleasant time in there.
The party stories started. I prepared for the men's
                                                   drinking.
And also . . . [*He breaks off*]
                    Are you listening? Don't doze off!

Finally, both S̲i̲k̲o̲n̲ and C̲h̲a̲i̲r̲e̲a̲s̲ contrast with Sostratos'
family retainer G̲e̲t̲a̲, a grim misogynistic crank for whom,
we must imagine, service in the city has more pains than
compensations. His recriminations are almost enough to convince us that he was born in the country and later migrated.

The theme of the city and the country, then, is handled
with considerable versatility on the level of characterization.
It was, of course, an incidental theme for Aristophanic Old
Comedy (cf. *Acharnians, Birds, Plutus*). But in Aristophanes,
the country serves as an idyllic or nostalgic escape from the
political and social evils of a city engulfed in war, taxes, and
other noisome obligations. In the *Dyskolos,* the theme is far
more fully explored. Nowhere is its development more
poignant, or more humorous, than in the characterization of
the protagonist, Knemon. And it is in Knemon, too, that we
can most clearly see Menander's painstaking individualization
of the stock "blocking character." Such individualization is,
in turn, linked with one aspect of the playwright's realism.

Introduced as a man who has exiled himself from humanity
(6), Knemon alternates between misanthropic rage and out-
bursts of self-pity in his short appearances up to Act Four.
His quirks are many. He diligently works his farm, yet throws
its fruits at intruders (121). He keeps a close eye on his
daughter, and has decided that only a man like himself will
marry her (335ff). He consistently alienates affection and
rejects the concern of others. Yet despite Knemon's meanness
and ill temper, Menander will not have us despise him totally.
The audience's interest and tolerance are sustained for the
first three acts by a caricature; then, suddenly, in Knemon's
apologia of Act Four (711ff), we learn that he is indeed a
thoroughly believable, and somewhat sympathetic human
being.

KNEMON [*irked, seeing* SOSTRATOS]

. . . . I think I've made just one mistake. That was
to feel that I alone was self-sufficient, and
would need no one. Now that I see how death can be
so swift and sudden, I know that I was wrong in this.
A man needs someone standing by to help him out.
I hadn't admitted that before, because I thought
that every man around cared only for his own
profit. By God, I thought there wasn't one of them
who was concerned for other men.
That was what blinded me. . . .
[*To* MYRRHINE]
Help me lie down, my girl. I think it's not a man's job
to say more than he has to. [*He sits up again*]
                                    But, child, I
want to add a bit about myself and how
I lived. If everyone lived so, there'd be no courts,
men wouldn't drag each other off to prison, war
would vanish—all would be content with modest lives.

This revelation is accomplished with no loss of credibility,
because it has been amply (though subtly) prepared for. In
the apologia, Knemon exhibits all the cantankerousness we
have come to expect of him. But he adds a credo which in
fact bears out the romantic speculations on nobility uttered
by Sostratos at 388–390. The youth imagines there that his
beloved has been "nurtured nobly in the country by her
father, who's a man that loathes life's evil ways." Indeed
Knemon does loathe life's evil ways, and has in his odd
fashion been motivated by something close to utopianism. Of
course, this is mingled with hypochondria, self-righteousness,
and the marvelously disingenuous self-pity that closes the
speech ("The difficult old *dyskolos* won't hinder you," 747).
Yet there is no reason why we should not take his admission of error and his generous, sensible dispositions for
the future at face value. That is, Knemon is capable of
admitting a mistake.

However, Menander is too much the realist to let it go at
that. For immediately after the great speech, Knemon reverts
to his old ways, in his sharp refusal to be introduced to

Sostratos, and in his grudging appraisal of the young man's
character through the observation that he is sunburned, as a
farmer should be (751ff). In Act Five, we see Knemon once
again as his old self, the grouch who blocks festivity, and we
are likely to remember as more significant, and ultimately
true to nature, his plea in the apologia: "If I survive . . . let
me live the way I want" (735–736). Did he only go through
the motions of a recantation so that he could insure he would
be left alone? We may now indeed suspect his motives, and
Menander probably intends for us to do so. But the outcome
supersedes this kind of suspicion: at the end Knemon is
brought willy-nilly to join the party. We may consider that
the very alternation between self-pity and irascibility, estab-
lished early in the play, forms the underpinning of Knemon's
speech in Act Four. Thus, his admission of error is set in the
context of the habits of a lifetime. The speech and its after-
math, then, exhibit a psychological realism which, for its
detail, is substantially new in Attic drama, and which goes far
beyond the "realism" of the *Characters* of Theophrastus. (On
the relation of these brief vignettes to Menander's plays, see
T. B. L. Webster, *An Introduction to Menander* 43ff and the
commentary of E. W. Handley, listed in the bibliography at
the end of this volume.) There is no passage of Aristophanes
which resembles Knemon's apologia in this respect. Once
again, Menander's closest analogue is Euripides. (Compare
particularly the great dramatic monologues of Phaedra and
Medea.)

This is the aspect of "realism" which most cogently validates
the ancient panegyrics of Menander's imitation of life. Other
features of Menander's work have been described as realistic:
the careful plot construction (he is, among other things, the
originator of the "well-made play"), the motivation of en-
trances and exits, the depiction of everyday middle-class life.
Yet these features, in themselves, would not suffice to ex-
plain why people went to the theater to see plays like the
Dyskolos. The neatness, logicality, and decorum of Menander's dramaturgy are symbolized by the famous story told
about him in Plutarch. As the time of the festival approached,

a friend is said to have asked the playwright about his progress. "I've completed the comedy," replied Menander; "the theme is sketched out: all I have to do is fill in the words." Coleridge would doubtless have called this method inorganic or mechanical form. Happily, the finished product, as we can judge it by the *Dyskolos* and *The Woman of Samos,* is not the artificial fabrication which the anecdote might suggest. However narrow the social milieu of the plays, Menander's psychological realism insures that his characters live. Beneath the surface repetitiveness of types is a subtly observant individualization, and beyond the bourgeois homogeneity of their world is the gently admonitory voice of a tolerant philosopher, whose vision sparkled at humanity's foibles.

III

The present translation seeks to present Menander's text in a readable version that is reasonably close to the original Greek. In several places, notably with proverbs and oaths, I have often departed from the original considerably and substituted modern equivalents. The iambic lines of varying length which I have used have their own decorum in English, and the language of the translation, as of the original, is doubtless more formal at many points than ordinary speech. On the other hand, the diction of several characters, especially Sikon and Chaireas, is more than once intentionally colloquial. I have not hesitated to depart from strict iambic rhythm when I have thought it desirable. As a general rule, the numbered lines of the translation correspond with the lines of the Greek text: if a verse is divided among speakers in Greek, it is similarly divided here in English also. An asterisk indicates that an explanatory note on the passage in question will be found at the end of this volume.

THE
DYSKOLOS

MENANDER

DRAMATIS PERSONAE

PAN, god of the woodlands
CHAIREAS, parasite of Sostratos
SOSTRATOS, son of Kallippides
PYRRHIAS, young slave of Sostratos
KNEMON, the *dyskolos*, an old farmer, father of Myrrhine
MYRRHINE, daughter of Knemon, beloved of Sostratos
DAOS, Gorgias' servant
GORGIAS, Knemon's stepson
SIKON, a cook
GETA, slave of Sostratos' family
SIMICHE, old servant of Knemon
MOTHER of Sostratos
KALLIPPIDES, father of Sostratos

SCENE

Phyle, a country district near Athens. In the center of the stage is the entrance to a cave, where a shrine, sacred to PAN and the Nymphs, is located. Two houses are at either side: stage right is the house of KNEMON, stage left the house of GORGIAS. The exit stage right leads to the fields, the exit stage left leads to the road to town.

PROLOGUE

[*Enter* PAN]

PAN

Our scene's the countryside, in Attica,
where farmers till the rocks for bread. This place
is Phyle. The Nymphs are famous here:
their sacred cave is right behind me.
On my right, the farm is owned by Knemon,   5
a man self-exiled from the human race:
an utter grouch and not gregarious.
That understates the case! He's over sixty
and refuses to enjoy a chat with anyone.
Because we're neighbors, he consents to greet me,   10
though this is an exception to his rule.
I'm sure he's promptly sorry he's been civil.
All the same, despite this temperament,
he got married to a widow. Her first husband
had just died and left behind a son: 15
the child was very young then.
The marriage was more like suing for divorce,
with sessions held all day and half the night.
Knemon nagged and was unhappy. When a little girl
was born, things went from bad to worse. When nothing
                                                  else   20
could change her bitter, dreary way of life,
his wife renounced the grouch, sought out her son
again, and lived with him. He owns a little
piece of land here, barely big enough

to feed himself, his mother, and a single   25
servant, faithful to the family.
The lad's turned out a fine young man,
who boasts a fund of sense beyond his years:
maturity comes easily when life goes hard.
Old Knemon grouches on, his solitude   30
intact but for his daughter and a servant hag.
He carries logs, and digs, and sweats,
and hates the world in order: starting here
with wife and neighbors, and going on for miles
down the road. A lonely childhood, though,   35
has kept his daughter innocent: piously
she tends this shrine. Her care of us inclines
my Nymphs and me to keep a special watch
on her. So, when a young man from the town,
whose father is extremely rich and owns   40
some large estates, came out to hunt here with
a friend, he chanced upon our neighborhood
and fell in love with Knemon's daughter. (You
might say a god had had a hand in it.)
These are the highlights: if you wish to see   45
the details (as I hope you do), you will.
Because I think I see the youthful lover
coming toward us with his fellow huntsman.
Their words will pick up just where I've left off.
[*Exit*]

ACT ONE

[*Enter* SOSTRATOS and CHAIREAS]

CHAIREAS

What, Sostratos? You saw a free-born girl who crowned   50
these statues of the Nymphs with flowers, and you fell
for her like that?

SOSTRATOS
At once.

CHAIREAS
                              Fast work. I'll bet
you left the house to fall in love on purpose!

SOSTRATOS
You're joking, Chaireas. I'm the one who's suffering.

CHAIREAS [*sarcastically*]
Oh, I believe it!

SOSTRATOS
                              I've brought you here with me   55
so you can help me. You're a friend, and very
practical.

CHAIREAS
                              Well, in such cases, Sostratos,
my strategies are these. A friend of mine

7

is horny for a whore: my plan's abduction.
I get loaded, burn her door down, am totally 60
irrational. I get him laid before
they're introduced. Delay can only swell
his love; a swift relief cures swift *amours.*
But say a friend plans marriage to a maiden,
I change my tack and do his homework for him. 65
I learn the background, income, personal details.
The way I fix things, any friend of mine
remembers me forever.

SOSTRATOS
          Sure he does—
[*aside*] but all this may not suit me.

CHAIREAS [*continuing right on*]
                    Now the first
requirement is for you to fill me in. 70

SOSTRATOS
I sent my hunting servant Pyrrhias out early . . .

CHAIREAS
Where to?

SOSTRATOS
          To meet the father of the girl,
or else to find her guardian,
whoever he may be.

CHAIREAS [*taken aback*]
              Good God,
you're kidding!

SOSTRATOS [*sheepishly*]
          I guess you're right. I shouldn't 75
have used a servant for that kind of thing.
But men in love don't often think so clearly.

I've been wondering for some time at his delay.
I told him to investigate things here
and then report directly back at home.   80
[*Enter* PYRRHIAS, *at a dead run*]

PYRRHIAS

Let me pass! Watch out! Get out of the way!
The madman's after me!

SOSTRATOS
What's this, boy?

PYRRHIAS

Clear out!

SOSTRATOS
What is it?

PYRRHIAS
He's throwing stones and mud at me!

I've had it!

SOSTRATOS
What? Where are you running, idiot?

PYRRHIAS [*stops short*]

You mean he's stopped?

SOSTRATOS
Of course!

PYRRHIAS
But I thought . . .

SOSTRATOS [*exasperated*]
What on earth   85

are you trying to say?

PYRRHIAS
>Let's get out of here!

SOSTRATOS
>*Where?*

PYRRHIAS [*shuddering, and pointing
to* KNEMON's *house*]
As far away as possible from that door!
Oh, he's the son of Woe! The man who lives
in there, the man you sent me to—he's crazy!
He's cracked! The devil's in him, he's . . . [*Breaks off*   90
>*with a grimace*]
OHHHH! My *toes*!! I think I've broken almost
all of them! I fell and . . .

SOSTRATOS [*to* CHAIREAS, *with a
gesture toward* PYRRHIAS]
>>Has he
gone mad, or done something he shouldn't?

CHAIREAS
He's obviously berserk.

PYRRHIAS [*still panting from his run*]
>No, no!!
Believe me, Sostratos! You must look out!   95
I ran so fast from him I'm out of breath.
[*Collecting himself*]
I knocked and said that I was looking for
the master. An old and bitchy servant came
to meet me, and she pointed out the place
he was—a little hill, where he was crawling round   100
where his wild pears grow, gathering
bits of wood . . .*

CHAIREAS
>How upset he is!
Do tell us what's the matter.

PYRRHIAS

I walked along
and came up near to him. I had in mind
to be extremely suave and tactful when 105
I spoke to him. "I beg your pardon, sir,"
I said, "I've come to see you on some business
which concerns you." He shot back, "You bastard,
you've come to trespass on my farm. What's
the idea? You have some nerve!" With that, 110
he threw a load of dirt right in my face!

CHAIREAS

The hell with him!

PYRRHIAS

I blinked and cursed him.
But then the old guy grabbed a stick and started
beating me. He shouted angrily,
"What business could we have together? Don't 115
you know the public road?"

CHAIREAS

This farmer
has to be completely nuts!

PYRRHIAS — *slave*

Then he
began to chase me, round the hill at first,
and then right down here through the brush, damn near
two miles. He pelted me with mud 120
and stones and, when all else had failed, with pears!
The job was a disaster—and the man's
a monster! I'm begging you, clear out!

SOSTRATOS

Coward!

PYRRHIAS

You don't know what we're up against. He'll eat us alive!

CHAIREAS

Perhaps the fellow is upset today.   125
Which leads me to believe it better
to postpone our visit, Sostratos.
My general rule for business is to wait
for the right moment.

PYRRHIAS [*to both of them*]
Be sensible.

CHAIREAS
A nasty
disposition's common to poor farmers: 130
he's typical. Tomorrow morning early
I'll come out and see him by myself
now that I know the place. For now, relax:
come home with me. I'll handle this for you.
[*Without waiting for* SOSTRATOS' *reaction,* CHAIREAS *exits*]

PYRRHIAS [*eagerly*]
Let's follow him.

SOSTRATOS [*bursts out*]
That faker? Why, he leaped   135
at an excuse to leave. Quite plainly from the start
he disapproved of marriage plans
and came with me reluctantly. But—YOU!
I'm damned if you don't get a whipping!

PYRRHIAS [*shocked*]
Why, what have I done wrong, Sostratos?   140

SOSTRATOS
You clearly broke some law here . . .

PYRRHIAS [*thinking he means theft*]
I swear I didn't take a thing.

SOSTRATOS
If that's
the truth, would he have beaten you?

PYRRHIAS [*staring offstage*]
He's here,
in person! I'm retreating, chief! You talk
to him. [PYRRHIAS *exits in a panic*]*

SOSTRATOS
I couldn't do that! I'm no good   145
at speeches. What am I to say to him?
He hardly looks the friendly sort.
He's bent on business. I'll
retreat a little from his door. That's better.
He's all alone, and shouting: perhaps he's mad?   150
By heaven, he's beginning to frighten me!
I'd be a liar if I didn't admit it.
[*Enter* KNEMON, *in a towering rage*]

KNEMON
Old Perseus was divinely favored—*twice!*
He had his wings and didn't have to meet
a single passerby. He also had   155
that thing to change the men who bothered him
to stone.* What a fine possession! I
wish I had it now——I'd convert
this place into a sculpture garden!
Life is unendurable, by heaven,   160
when chattering strangers trespass on your land!
You'd think, by God, I *liked* to waste my time
along the highway! Well, I've given up working
on this section of the farm. Too many people
bother me. Just now they've chased right up the hill   165
to get at me! God damn these wretched mobs!!
[*Sees* SOSTRATOS]
Someone's here again—standing right
at my front door!

SOSTRATOS [*to himself*]
I wonder if he'll hit me.

KNEMON
The situation's desperate: a man
can't even be alone to hang himself!   170

SOSTRATOS [*addressing him*]
Please don't be angry at me, sir. I'm waiting
for a friend here.

KNEMON [*rhetorically*]
                You see what I was saying?
[*To* SOSTRATOS] You think this property's the public
                                                square?
[*Ironically*] If you've arranged appointments at my
                                                house,
you should provide for greater comfort. [*His voice
            rising*] Why not   175
install a chair here? [*Shouts*] Or, even better, build
a *meeting room*? [*Desperate*] This confounded insolence!
It plagues my life! My life's a living hell!
[*Exits into his house*]

SOSTRATOS
It's pretty clear that this affair is not
to be a casual effort; it's going to need   180
some nerve. I think I'll go see Geta, Father's
slave. The very man I need, in fact:
he's got imagination, and he's most
experienced in every sort of planning.
I know he'll have a way to change the old   185
man's mood. [*Pauses, then to himself*] Let's not lose
                                                time!
A lot might come of this, just in
a single day. [*A noise is heard at the door of* KNEMON's *house*]
                But someone's coming out.
[*Enter* KNEMON's *daughter*]*

MYRRHINE

Oh, heavens, what an awful thing has happened!
What will I do? The nurse has gone and dropped   190
our bucket down the well!

SOSTRATOS [*transfixed*]
Gods above,
Apollo, Castor, Pollux! Heal me—save me!
What beauty!

MYRRHINE [*still to herself*]
When he went out, my father
told me to heat some water . . .

SOSTRATOS [*to the audience*]
She's marvelous!

MYRRHINE [*distracted*]
He'll beat her to a pulp if he should learn   195
what's happened. I've got no time to waste—
dearest Nymphs, I must borrow water from you.
[*hesitates*] I'd be ashamed, though, to disturb the prayers
of anyone inside the shrine . . .

SOSTRATOS [*addressing her*]
If I may,
I'd be delighted to fetch the water for you.   200

MYRRHINE [*eagerly*]
Oh, yes—please do! [*She gives him a jug*]

SOSTRATOS [*to himself, as he moves
toward the cave*]
She's from the country, but
she's so well mannered! Can any of the honored gods
save me now from love? [*He exits into the shrine just
as a noise is heard*]

MYRRHINE
                              Oh, Lord,
what was that noise? Is Father coming out?
I'll catch a beating if he finds me here   205
outside.
[DAOS *enters from* GORGIAS' *house. He is speaking to*
GORGIAS' *mother, inside.*]

DAOS
                    I can't keep sitting here with you
while Gorgias has to dig alone.
I'll have to help him.
[*He turns away from the door, and says to himself*]
                              Damn you, poverty!
Why is it that we're always poor?
Our bad luck's like a guest who comes to visit   210
and who won't go away.
[*Sostratos reenters from the shrine, bearing the water*]

SOSTRATOS [*to* MYRRHINE]
                         I've brought the water back
for you.

MYRRHINE [*motioning him toward*
KNEMON's *door*]   Please, over here.

DAOS [*to himself*]
                         What can this man
be up to?

SOSTRATOS [*to* MYRRHINE]
             Good-bye! Look after your father.
[*Exit* MYRRHINE, *into* KNEMON's *house.* SOSTRATOS *looks after
her, and says to himself*]
Oh, lord, I'm miserable! [*He gathers himself together*]
                         Stop moaning, Sostratos.
It's going to be all right.

DAOS [*eavesdropping, to himself*]
How's that?

SOSTRATOS [*still to himself*]
                          Don't worry.   215
Return with Geta, as you planned just now—
and tell him everything that's happened here.
[*Exit* SOSTRATOS]

DAOS [*suspiciously*]
I'm ill-at-ease about this business.
In fact, I don't approve of it at all!
This lad is doing favors for a girl—suspicious!   220
Knemon should rot in hell for this!
He leaves his little girl here all alone
and takes no proper care to guard her.
It's likely that the young man heard of this
and sneaked up here to take advantage of   225
a windfall. Clearly I will have to tell her brother,
as quickly as I can, in order that
we both may see about protecting her.
I think I'd better go right now,
because I see a group of somewhat drunken   230
worshipers of Pan carousing toward us.
I'd just as soon avoid their revelry. [*Exit*]

[Choral Interlude]*

ACT TWO

[*Enter* GORGIAS *and* DAOS, *in the middle of a conversation*]

GORGIAS
From what you've said of this affair, Daos,
you handled it too casually.

DAOS
How's that?

GORGIAS
By God, you should have pinned the man right on   235
the spot, whoever he was, and warned him not
to try a thing like that again! But, as it is,
you backed away from everything, just like
a stranger. You can't just shuck off family
obligations, Daos. My sister's still   240
our obligation, though her father keeps
avoiding us. But let's not imitate
his grumpiness. Besides, if shame should come
upon my sister, the blame is also mine.
Outside the family, gossips never know   245
who did it. All they know is that it's done.

DAOS*
But Master Gorgias, I'm absolutely scared
to death of the old man. He'll string me up
directly if he finds me at
his door.

GORGIAS [*reflectively*]
  He is a problem, I admit.   250
Converting him to better ways is difficult:
we can't convince him by reproaching him.
The law's on his side if we force him, and
his grouchy temper turns aside persuasion.

DAOS [*staring offstage*]
Hold on a bit. We haven't come in vain. 255
As I predicted, our man's come back.
[*Enter* SOSTRATOS]

GORGIAS
You mean that one who's wearing fancy clothes?

DAOS
That's him!

GORGIAS
  A rascal, judging by his looks.

SOSTRATOS [*to himself*]
I couldn't locate Geta at my house.
My mother's getting ready for a sacrifice— 260
I don't know which—she's always at her prayers,
parading round the town performing them.
She's sent our servant out to hire some chef.
I wasn't going to get involved in that
affair. I thought it best to come back here. 265
The time has to come to speak out for myself.
No more pacing back and forth. I'll knock.
Once I do that, my second thoughts won't count.

GORGIAS [*steps up to him*]
I have a pretty serious thing to say
to you, my friend. Please listen.

SOSTRATOS
    Gladly. What's the matter? 270

GORGIAS

It's my opinion that the luck of every
man is bound to change, no matter if
he's doing well or just the opposite;
and if a man is lucky, he'll only stay
that way as long as he can manage his   275
affairs without unjustly harming others.
When his fortunate position leads
him to injustice, then he can expect
some changes in his fortune for the worse.
A man who's doing badly, though, may find   280
a better share in life, if in his plight
he lives uprightly, bears his fate with simple
courage, and is admired for his integrity.
What's all this mean? I wouldn't feel too smug
about your wealth, if I were you. Don't come   285
and injure us, the poor. But rather show
to others you deserve the wealth you have.

SOSTRATOS [*puzzled*]
You think I'm doing something wrong right now?

GORGIAS [*bluntly*]
You thought you'd get away with something cheap.   290
You planned to lure a free-born girl to sin,
or watch for opportunity to do a thing
you'd pay for with your life!

SOSTRATOS [*shocked*]
                    My God!

GORGIAS [*sententiously*]
                                It's hardly
fair for you to use your leisure
to trouble those who have to work. Remember:
an injured man who's poor is hard to handle.   295
The public's on his side, and he believes
that you've assaulted him, not simply pushed him.

SOSTRATOS [*earnestly*]

I wish your lot were better, friend! But now
please hear my side . . .

DAOS [*interrupting*]
                           Master, that was quite   300
a speech. Well done!*

SOSTRATOS [*reprovingly*]
                           You too, you chatterer!
I saw a certain girl here. I'm in love
with her. If this is wrong, I guess I'm guilty.
What else am I to say? Except that I
have come here not to her, but so that I   305
may meet her father. Since I'm free by birth
and have enough to live on, I'm prepared
to ask her hand without a dowry, pledging
eternal love. [*Solemnly*] If I came here intent
on evil, or to do to you some secret   310
harm, my friend, may Pan here and his Nymphs
avenge the deed by striking me right down
beside this house. I'm terribly upset
that you believed me less than honorable.

GORGIAS [*impressed*]

Well, if for my part I was more abrupt   315
than necessary, I apologize.
Your words convince me. You have me as your friend.
My man, I spoke to you not as a stranger:
I'm kin to her. The girl is my half-sister.

SOSTRATOS [*brightly*]

That's great! You'll be a help in what I plan!   320

GORGIAS

How so?

SOSTRATOS

You seem to be a generous man.

GORGIAS

I hardly want to put you off with vain
excuses, but I'll tell you how things are.
She's got a father like no other human
being who ever lived.

SOSTRATOS [*ironically*]
                                    I think I know   325
his temper.

GORGIAS
                    Trouble's not the word for it.
This farm he has would sell for quite a sum,
I think. But he refuses to employ a soul,
and works it all alone. He won't take on
a servant in the house, or hire a man: 330
he has no neighbor to disturb his solitude.
For him the nicest thing is seeing nobody.
He works most often with his daughter at
his side; he'll talk to her, but only her.
He finds it hard to chat with other people.   335
He says he'll marry her to any man
he finds who's like himself.

SOSTRATOS [*gloomily*]
                                    But that's
never!

GORGIAS
                    Friend, I wish you wouldn't get
involved. It's useless. Leave us be. We are
the ones who have to deal with this bad luck.   340

SOSTRATOS

But tell me, man, have you ever been in love?

GORGIAS

I can't imagine it.

SOSTRATOS
                    Why not?
Who's stopping you?

GORGIAS
                    A realistic look
at hardship, which is all I have in life.

SOSTRATOS
You certainly don't sound as if you've been   345
in love. You tell me to give up. But that's
no longer in my power.

GORGIAS
We don't resent you, but your carrying on is useless.

SOSTRATOS
Not if I win the girl.

GORGIAS
                    But you can't win.*
I'll prove that to you if you follow me   350
to where he's working. It's a valley near to us.

SOSTRATOS
What are you going to do?

GORGIAS
                    I'll just
drop in a word about his daughter's wedding;
I'd gladly witness the event myself.
Right off he'll raise objections to a match,   355
reviling one and all. The sight of you,
a gentleman of leisure, will revolt him.

SOSTRATOS
He's there right now?

GORGIAS
                Oh, no. He'll go
a little later by his same old route.

SOSTRATOS
He'll take the girl, you think?

GORGIAS
                        It's hard to say.   360
Maybe.

SOSTRATOS
                I'm ready! Bring me to the place.
And, I entreat you, take my side.

GORGIAS
                                How so?

SOSTRATOS
How so? Let's go there and you'll see.

DAOS [*interrupting*]
                                Hold on!
You're going to stand around in fancy clothes
while we're at work?

SOSTRATOS
                Why not?

DAOS
                        He'll start at once   365
to throw mud at you and curse you out
as idle. You'll have to dig with us. Perhaps
he'll venture then to hear a word from you,
believing you're a poor, small farmer, hard
at work.

SOSTRATOS
I'll do what you suggest. Lead on.   370
[*He starts taking off his cloak*]

GORGIAS [*half to himself*]
Why force yourself to suffer?

DAOS [*slyly, aside to* GORGIAS]
I've a plan:
we'll work today as hard as possible.
This guy will sprain his back, and then we won't
be bothered in the future with his visits.

SOSTRATOS [*turning back to them*]
Bring out a mattock for me.

DAOS
Here—take mine.   375
I've got to see to building up the fence.
It needs some work.

SOSTRATOS
Fine. Give it here to me.
[*To* GORGIAS] You've saved me.

DAOS [*to* GORGIAS]
Master, see you there. I'm off.
[*Exit* DAOS]

SOSTRATOS [*continuing*]
You see, I'm going to marry her, or else
I'll die!

GORGIAS
If that's the way you really feel,   380
I wish you luck. [*Exit*]

SOSTRATOS [*euphorically*]
                    Oh, honored gods! Friend,
the very things which you supposed would turn
me back have doubly spurred me on to act.
To get the girl would be stupendous,
if she's been raised outside the company   385
of women, and if she's innocent of evil.
She's not been terrified by any aunt
or nurse, but rather nurtured nobly in
the country by her father, who's a man that loathes
life's evil ways. [*Pauses*] This mattock weighs a ton.   390
It's going to kill me—but I'll have to see
this through, now that I've started on the way. [*Exit*]
[*Enter* SIKON, *dragging a sheep for the sacrifice*]

SIKON

This sheep's no ordinary beauty! Devil
take it. If I pick it up, it grabs
a tree branch in its mouth and starts to eat   395
the leaves; that way it pulls itself right off
my shoulder. If it's on the ground, it won't
move on. A paradox! The *sheep* is chopping me,
the cook, to pieces. I'd rather drag a sailboat
down the road.* Thank God, we've come at last   400
to where we've got to sacrifice. [*Nods toward the
                                  shrine*] Greetings,
Pan. [*Sees* GETA, *offstage, and calls to him*]
                So far behind?
[*Enter* GETA, *staggering under a heavy load of baggage*]

GETA
                Those blasted women
piled me with a load to carry that
would make four donkeys sweat.

SIKON
                    It looks as if
a large-ish crowd is coming. You've a raft   405
of rugs for them to sit on!

                    GETA [*inquiring where he is to put
his load*]

                    What . . . ?*

                    SIKON [*gesturing*]
                        Right here.

                    GETA
Done. [*He drops the baggage*] I'm certain, if she had a
                                        dream
of Pan in Paiania,* we'd be off
at once to sacrifice.

                    SIKON [*curious*]
                    Who had a dream?

                    GETA [*wearily*]
Don't bug me.

                    SIKON
                    Oh come on, Geta, tell.   410
Who had it?

                    GETA
                    Mistress had it.

                    SIKON
                        What'd she see?

                    GETA [*impatient*]
You'll kill me. Well, she saw the god . . .

SIKON

You mean Pan here?

GETA

... that's right ...

SIKON

Do what?

GETA

... take Master Sostratos ...

SIKON

A fine young man ...

GETA

... and clap him into chains ...

SIKON

Good God!

GETA

... and then equip him with a farmer's   415
cloak and mattock, and order him to work
the neighbor's land.

SIKON [*amazed*]
How strange!

GETA

We're sacrificing
because of this bad omen.

SIKON
I understand. [*All business now*] Grab up this stuff again
and take it in. Let's get the couches ready   420
and make the other preparations. We'll
be all set whenever they come. I hope

it all goes well. Cheer up, you pessimist!
I'll fill you up with gourmet food today.

GETA

I've always liked you and admired your skill—   425
[*Aside*] But I'll believe the food when it's in front of me.
[*They exit into the shrine*]

[Choral Interlude]

ACT THREE

[*Enter* KNEMON, *talking to* SIMICHE *the maid as he comes out the door*]

KNEMON

Old woman, shut the door and lock it tight
till I get back again. I don't think that
will be until it's after dark.
[*Enter* SOSTRATOS' *mother, with a large party of servants and guests*]

MOTHER*
Addressing SOSTRATOS' *sister,* PLANGON]
Move on quickly, Plangon. We should have done   430
the sacrifice by now.

KNEMON [*staring at them*]
What's going on?
A crowd! To hell with them!

MOTHER [*to a maid*]
Parthenis, pipe
the song of Pan. They say one shouldn't pray
in silence to this god.
[*Enter* GETA, *from the shrine*]

GETA
You got here safely!

30

KNEMON

By God, they really nauseate me!

GETA

We've 435

been waiting here for you some time.

MOTHER

Is all

in order for the sacrifice?

GETA

Oh, yes. All set.

MOTHER

That sheep, at least, won't wait around much longer.
Poor thing, it's almost dead. Well, go inside.
Prepare the baskets, holy water, and
the sacred cakes. 440
[*They all start to make their way into the cave*]

GETA [*as he leaves, seeing* KNEMON]
What are you gaping at? [*Exit*]

KNEMON [*outraged*]
God damn you all! They're making me fall idle!
I can't be off and leave the house with them
around. These Nymphs are nuisances as neighbors.
I'll have to tear the house down—build again 445
some other place. These people sacrifice like thieves!
They bring their picnic baskets, bottles—not for
the gods, but for themselves. A proper gift
for gods is holy incense and a cake:
the god gets all the offering when it's burned. 450
But these men give the gods
a sheep's tail and a bladder, parts which they
can't eat, and then they gobble up the rest.
[*Moves to his front door*]
Woman, open up the door at once.

I think we'll have to work inside today. [*Exit*]   455
[*Enter* GETA *from the shrine*]

                    GETA [*to the servants inside*]
You say you left the stewing pot behind?
You must all be hung over. Now what do we do?
[*Moves toward* KNEMON's *house*]
I guess I'll have to bother the god's neighbors.
[*Knocks at* KNEMON's *door*]
Hey, there, inside: boy! [*Mutters to himself*] By heavens,
                                    I'm sure
there's nothing worse than those repulsive slave   460
girls in the cave. [*Turns back to the door and
     knocks*] Servants—hey! [*As before*] Getting laid is all
they think about . . . Hey, there, inside, come out!! . . .
and slandering all who catch them at it . . . Boy!
What's going on here? Slaves! There's not a soul
inside. [*Listens at the door*] Ah, now there's someone
                              coming out.   465
[*Enter* KNEMON, *furious*]

                         KNEMON
You thrice accursed being, why's your hand
upon my door? Speak up!

                         GETA [*stepping back*]
                Don't bite!

                         KNEMON
                        I'll bite
and eat you too, God damn it!

                         GETA
                Good lord, calm down!

                         KNEMON
You wretch, have you and I got business with
each other?

GETA

      Oh, no, no business. Look—I haven't 470
brought a witness: I'm not collecting debts.*
I've come to ask you for a stewing pot.

KNEMON [*incredulous*]

A stewing pot?

GETA
      A pot.

KNEMON
      You ought to get a whipping!
You think I've got an ox to sacrifice,
the way you people do?

GETA [*aside*]
      You probably 475
don't have a snail. [*Hastily*] Good-bye, good sir.
               The girls
inside the shrine requested me to knock
upon your door and ask. I did. You have no pots.
I'll tell them that when I get back.
      [*Muttering, as he leaves*] Gods above!
The old man bites just like a snake! [*Exit*] 480

KNEMON

Wild animals, they are! They come right up
and knock as if you were a friend. [*Turns toward
              the shrine*] If I
catch any man come to my door, and don't
make an example out of him, then
count me as a nobody. I don't 485
know how this guy got off so well just now. [*Exit*]
[*Enter* SIKON *from the shrine; he is speaking over
his shoulder to* GETA, *inside*]

SIKON ~ ~~speaks~~

The hell with you! You say he swore at you?
You probably were rude to him. [*Turns away from
                              the cave*] It's clear
that most men cannot handle things like this.
I've got some skill at them. My customers in town   490
are legion, and I borrow stuff from neighbors
all the time. It takes a little buttering up.
For instance, if an older chap
comes to the door, at once I say, "Dear sir."
An old hag gets "Madame." In middle   495
age they're called "Priestess." A servant should
be flattered thus: "Good man," or "My dear boy."
The people in the shrine are crude; they should be whipped.
        [*Knocks at* KNEMON's *door*] Hey, boys!
[KNEMON *appears at his doorway*]
Come out, dear sir, I'd like to speak with you.

                    KNEMON [*if anything, angrier than
before*]
You're back? Again?

                    SIKON [*taken aback*]
            Oh boy, what's this?

                    KNEMON
                              It seems   500
you're riling me on purpose. Didn't I say
to you to keep away? [*Calls inside*] Old woman, bring
                              the whip!
[KNEMON *grabs hold of* SIKON]

                    SIKON [*struggling*]
Let go of me!

                    KNEMON [*sarcastically*]
        Let go?

SIKON
Please, sir, stop!

[SIKON *breaks free*]

KNEMON [*snarling at him*]
Come back for more!

SIKON [*starting to swear*]
May God . . .

KNEMON [*interrupting*]
You're jabbering still?

SIKON [*calming down a little*]
I came to ask you for a casserole.   505

KNEMON [*enraged*]
I haven't *got* a casserole—or knife,
or salt, or vinegar, or anything.
I've *told* you all to keep away from me.

SIKON
You didn't tell *me*.

KNEMON
I'm telling you now!

SIKON [*aside*]
Worse luck for you. [*To* KNEMON] Well, couldn't you tell   510
me where
I'd find someone to lend it to me?

KNEMON
I knew it!
Still chattering at me?

SIKON
Many thanks! Good-bye.

KNEMON

I don't need any farewell words from you!

SIKON

I take them back then!

KNEMON [*grumbling as he turns
to go back into his house*] Insufferable! [*Exit*]

SIKON

He's pounded
me to bits—and I was so polite!   515
A lot of difference *that* makes. Do I try
again? It won't be easy if all the people here
are going to use me as a punching bag.
[*Pondering*] Why don't I roast the meat? I will. I've got
a broiling pan. Meanwhile, so long to the Phylasians!   520
I don't need them. I'll make do with what I have. [*Exit*]
[*Enter* SOSTRATOS, *weary and disheveled*]

SOSTRATOS*

Whoever needs more problems, let him come
to hunt in Phyle! Oh! I'm done for:
my lower back, my shoulders, and my neck—
all over! Right away I fell to work,   525
being young and strong. I swung the mattock way
up high and struck in deep, like any pro.
The work went well, but not for very long.
I started turning round a bit to see
if the old man was coming up, together   530
with his daughter. I rubbed my back a little,
while the others weren't looking. But when
the work dragged on, I started stretching backwards:
I was as stiff as wood. Still no one came.
The sun beat down. And finally   535
I looked just like a crane—was scarcely
bending up and then, with my whole body,
going down again. When he saw me,

Gorgias said, "It doesn't look as if
he'll come today, my friend." "What then?" I said   540
at once. "Shall we leave off—come back tomorrow?"
Daos took over for me. That's the story of
my first attempt. I cannot tell you why
on earth I've come back here, but I am drawn
back to this place like some automaton.   545
[*Enter* GETA *from the shrine; he speaks over his
shoulder to* SIKON, *inside*]

GETA

Come on, now, man! You think I'm blessed with sixty hands?
I light the grill for you, I take
the innards of the sheep . . . do carrying, washing,
chopping . . .* I knead the cakes, bring round the pots . . .
The smoke in there is blinding me!   550
[*Sarcastically*] I'm having a real holiday!

SOSTRATOS

Hey, Geta!

GETA [*still not seeing him*]

Who's calling?

SOSTRATOS

I am.

GETA

Who?

SOSTRATOS

You see me?

GETA

Yes!

It's Master.

SOSTRATOS
Tell me what you're doing here.

GETA
You're asking "What?" We've done the sacrifice and are
preparing lunch for you.

SOSTRATOS
My mother's here?   555

GETA
Oh, yes.

SOSTRATOS
And father?

GETA
He's expected. Go inside.

SOSTRATOS
I've got an errand first. [*Thinking out loud*] It's lucky
                                                that
the sacrifice took place here. I'll invite
the farmer Gorgias without delay,
and also Daos. When they've joined with us   560
in celebrating, they'll be even better
allies. They'll help me win the girl.

GETA [*overhearing*]
What's that? You're off to bring some more to lunch?
[*Ironically*] Well, go ahead! As far as I'm concerned,
invite three thousand! I was well aware   565
I'd not get anything to eat. How could I?
Go on, invite the world! You've just killed off
a beauty of a sheep. You think those charming
women would share a thing with me inside? Not on
your life. They wouldn't part with grains of salt!   570

SOSTRATOS

Don't worry, Geta. Today will turn out fine.
[*Turns toward the shrine*]
I'll prophesy that by myself, O Pan.
Of course, I always greet you, and respect you.* [*Exit*]
[*Enter from* KNEMON's *house* SIMICHE, *the maid; she is distraught*]

SIMICHE

Oh trouble, trouble, triple trouble's mine!*

GETA

Oh, devil take it! Some old woman's come out   575
the grouch's door.

SIMICHE [*as before*]
                    What will I have to suffer?
I tried to get the bucket from the well
without my master's knowing . . .
I tied his mattock to a little rope . . .
It was too weak and rotten— and   580
it broke on me!!

GETA [*ironically*]
            Good show!

SIMICHE
                    So now—poor me!
I've let the bucket *and* the mattock drop!

GETA

There's one thing left to do: jump in yourself!

SIMICHE

And Knemon wants the mattock, just by chance,
to move some dung in the yard.* He's running round   585
looking for it and shouting . . .
[*A noise is heard at the door;* SIMICHE *freezes in terror*]
                    God, that's him!

GETA

Run for your life, you wretched woman! Run!
[*Enter* KNEMON]
Too late! Defend yourself!

KNEMON [*enraged*]
Where is that thief?

SIMICHE [*cowering*]

Oh, master! It was an accident!

KNEMON
Go on inside!

SIMICHE

Oh, tell me what you're going to do?   590

KNEMON [*savagely*]

DO? I'm going to tie you up . . .

SIMICHE [*shrieks*]
Oh, no!

KNEMON

And use that same old rope to drop you down!

GETA

Bravo! If the rope is really rotten.

SIMICHE

Shall I call Daos from next door to help?

KNEMON

Call Daos, wretch, now that you've ruined me?   595
I told you once. Get in the house! Go on!
[*Exit* SIMICHE. KNEMON *sighs to himself*]
Oh, dear. I'm utterly forsaken now!*

Like no one else! I shall go down the well:
what else is there to do?

GETA [*addressing him*]
               We'll give you a rope
and hook.

KNEMON [*turning on him*]
          May all the gods give *you* damnation,   600
if you talk nonsense to me like that! [*Exit*]

GETA

I'd deserve it, too. He's rushed inside
again, the wretched fellow. What a life!
The quintessential Attic countryman:
he fights the rocks, which bear him thyme and sage.   605
Hardship's his lot, and he gets nothing for it.
[*Looking offstage, he sees* SOSTRATOS *approaching*]
But here's the master coming toward us with
his guests in tow. [*Looking more closely, he is amazed*]
             They're laborers from round
the district here! How out of place this is.
Why bring them over now? Where _did_   610
he get to know them? [*Exit into the cave*]*
[*Enter* SOSTRATOS, GORGIAS, *and* DAOS]

SOSTRATOS

I wouldn't hear of a refusal. We've
got quite enough to go around. By God,
who in the world can say he will not come
to lunch when his friend's just made a sacrifice?
For, I assure you, long before we met   615
I was your friend. [*He turns to the servant*]
             Take in these tools, Daos,
and then come back.

GORGIAS [*to* DAOS]
                You can't leave Mother all alone.
Go in and see to what she needs.
I'll come right back myself in just a minute.
[*Exit* DAOS *to* GORGIAS' *house.* SOSTRATOS *and* GORGIAS
go into the shrine]

[Choral Interlude]

ACT FOUR

[*Enter* SIMICHE *from* KNEMON's *house; she is distraught*]

SIMICHE

Oh God, what misery! Can someone help us?   620
Oh, please help!
[*Enter* SIKON *from the shrine*]

SIKON
                Damn it! Will you,
by all that's holy, let us pour our drinks*
in peace? You shout at us, you beat us, now
you wail at us. Your household's downright weird!

SIMICHE

The master's down the well!

SIKON
                What's that?

SIMICHE
                                I'm telling you—   625
he went to get the mattock and the bucket,
and then he slipped, and now he's fallen in!
Right down the well!

SIKON
                You don't mean him—
the grouch? By God, that's good! I'm glad.
My dear old lady, now it's up to you.   630

43

SIMICHE

What should I do?

SIKON
Go find a rock, a heavy bowl,
or anything like that, and throw it down on him!

SIMICHE

Oh, please, go down and save him!

SIKON

Go fight a rabid dog inside a well?* Not me.

SIMICHE [*desperately*]
Oh, Gorgias, wherever are you?
[*Enter* GORGIAS *from the shrine*]

GORGIAS
Here!   635
What's the matter, Simiche?

SIMICHE
I've just
been telling him. My master's down the well!

GORGIAS [*shouting inside*]
Come out here, Sostratos! [*To* SIMICHE] Quick! Show the way.
[SOSTRATOS *rushes out from the cave, and follows* GORGIAS
and SIMICHE *into* KNEMON's *house*]

SIKON [*gleefully*]
The gods are really up there, after all!
[*Shakes his fist at* KNEMON's *door*]
So you begrudge a stewing pot to those   640
who sacrifice, you rogue! You've fallen in now:
drink up your water, then, so you don't have
to share it with a soul! [*Turns back*] The Nymphs have
                                    punished him

just now for me, and justly. You can't
insult a chef and get away with it! 645
There's something sanctified about our art.
Of course, a waiter's less important. You
can treat him any way you want.

   [*Listens at* KNEMON's *door*] He can't be dead.
There's someone crying "Daddy!" . . .* 649
      . . . What a sight 656
do you think he'll be, by God! Drenched from his dip,
all shivering. A pretty picture! [*To the audience*] I'll
just love to see it, friends!
[*He calls into the shrine*]
Start pouring out an offering, girls, but change the
         prayer to this: 660
"May the old man be rescued, as a cripple
with mutilated legs!" That way he won't
be able to annoy the god his neighbor,
or bother those who sacrifice. If I get hired
again to cook, I'll want him out of action. 665
[*Exit into the shrine. Enter* SOSTRATOS *from* KNEMON's *house*]

SOSTRATOS

By all the gods, men, I have never seen
before a man who just missed drowning at
a more attractive time!
I've had a marvelous adventure there!
When we rushed in, young Gorgias at once 670
sprang down the well, while Knemon's girl
remained with me around the top. What else
were we to do? Except that she began
to tear her hair, to moan, to strike her breast.
And I, the golden boy, stood by her, just 675
as if I were her nurse, and begged her not
to grieve like that. I looked at her as on
a splendid work of art. I couldn't have cared
about the injured man below, except
I had to keep on hauling at the rope. 680
I nearly was the death of him, in fact.

While looking at her, I let go the rope,
about three times! But Gorgias was splendid.
He really outdid Atlas! He held, and got
him up at last. With Knemon safe, I came   685
out here. I really couldn't keep a hold
on my emotions any longer.
I nearly went and kissed her: that's the way
I feel! Right now, I'm going to . . .
[*A noise is heard at* KNEMON's *door*]
                                             Here they are!
[*Enter* KNEMON, MYRRHINE, *and* GORGIAS.* SOSTRATOS *stares*
at MYRRHINE]
Oh, Zeus, deliver me! What a sight!*   690

                          GORGIAS [*kindly*]
Tell me, Knemon, if you want anything.

                          KNEMON [*weakly*]
What's that? I'm ill.

                          GORGIAS
                          Take heart.

                          KNEMON
                                   Oh, it's all right.
Old Knemon won't annoy you any more
in the future.

                          GORGIAS
                   Such misfortune is the price
of being alone, you know. You nearly died   695
just now. A man your age has got to live
with a companion.

                          KNEMON
                   Gorgias, I'm not
too well, I know. Go quickly, call your mother.
[*Exit* GORGIAS *to his own house*]

It seems we only learn our lessons when
we suffer some bad accident.   700
[*To* MYRRHINE] Little girl, please hold me up.

SOSTRATOS [*enviously*]
Oh, lucky man!

KNEMON [*irked, seeing* SOSTRATOS]
You wretch, why are you standing there?*   702
                          . . . Not one of you   711
could make me change my mind. You'll have to let me have
my way. I think I've made just one mistake. That was
to feel that I alone was self-sufficient and
would need no one. Now that I see how death can be   715
so swift and sudden, I know that I was wrong in this.
A man needs someone standing by to help him out.
I hadn't admitted that before, because I thought
that every man around cared only for his own
profit. By God, I thought there wasn't one of them   720
who was concerned for other men. That was what blinded me.
One man has just now proved the opposite:
Gorgias, who's done a deed that's worthy of
the finest gentleman. I never let him near
my door, or gave him help in anything,   725
or greeted or conversed with him, and still he saved me.
Another man might well have said: "You don't allow
me in—well, I won't come. You've never helped us out—
I won't help you." [*Catches sight of* GORGIAS, *who has
now returned, and looks embarrassed*]
                     What's the matter, boy? If I
should die—I think that's likely, seeing as how I feel— 730
or whether I live, I'm making you my legal son,
and heir to what I own. It's yours. And take the girl:
she's in your care. Find her a man. For even if
I live, I won't be able to. Not a single one
will ever please me. If I survive, though, let   735
me live the way I want. Do all else as you wish.
Thank God, you're sensible. You're just the man to be

your sister's guardian. Give half of my estate
as dowry for her; the rest can feed me and your mother.
[*To* MYRRHINE]
Help me lie down, my girl. I think it's not a man's   740
job to say more than he has to. [*He sits up again*]
                              But, child, I
want to add a bit about myself and how
I lived. If everyone lived so, there'd be no courts,
men wouldn't drag each other off to prison, war
would vanish—all would be content with modest lives.   745
[*To the audience*]
But your ways suit you better, doubtless. So, live on.
[*Almost to himself, with some self-pity*]
The difficult old *dyskolos* won't hinder you.

GORGIAS

I'll see to everything. If you agree, though, you
must help us quickly find a bridegroom for the girl.

KNEMON [*very much his old self*]
Look here! I've said what I intended! Can't you leave me?   750

GORGIAS [*gesturing toward*
SOSTRATOS]
This man would like to meet you . . .

KNEMON [*sharply*]
                    Absolutely not!

GORGIAS

He helped to save you.

KNEMON [*pausing*]
Oh. Who's that?

GORGIAS
            Right here. [*He beckons
to* SOSTRATOS] Come on!

KNEMON [*looking* SOSTRATOS *over*]
He's sunburned . . . He's a farmer, eh?

GORGIAS [*eagerly*]
         Oh yes, Father.
He's not a wealthy idler, wasting time all day . . .*   755

KNEMON
Wheel me in now.   758
[*Exeunt* KNEMON *and his family*]*

SOSTRATOS [*to* GORGIAS]
My father won't object to this.

GORGIAS
         Then, Sostratos,   761
I give her to you in betrothal, here
before the gods as witnesses. You deserve her.*
You came to us with no put-on emotion, but
sincerely, and you've thought it right to go all out   765
to marry her. Brought up in luxury, you willingly
worked on the farm. It's this way most of all that true
men are revealed: if someone rich should undertake
to imitate the poor. A man like this will bear
a change in fortune bravely. You have proved your
                        worth.   770
May you maintain it.

SOSTRATOS [*rather pleased with
himself*] I'll be even better yet!
[*Pauses*] I guess to praise oneself is somewhat vulgar, though,
[*He looks offstage*] But here's my father! What luck!

GORGIAS [*looking off in the same
direction*] Kallippides?
Is *he* your father?

SOSTRATOS

Sure.

GORGIAS [*impressed*]

By heaven, he's awfully rich!
And he deserves it—quite a farmer!
[*Enter* KALLIPPIDES]

KALLIPPIDES

I appear   775
to be too late. They've surely eaten up the sheep
by now and gone back to the farm.

GORGIAS [*to* SOSTRATOS]

He looks as if
he's starving. Shall we approach him now?

SOSTRATOS

No, let him eat.
He'll be in better spirits.

KALLIPPIDES [*seeing* SOSTRATOS]

Sostratos, you've eaten?

SOSTRATOS [*nodding*]

But there's some left for you. Go in.

KALLIPPIDES

I will indeed.   780
[*He exits into the shrine*]

GORGIAS

You'll want to talk to him in private now. Go on inside.

SOSTRATOS [*pointing at* KNEMON's
house]
You'll wait for me in there, all right?

GORGIAS

I won't go out.

SOSTRATOS
I'll call you right away.
[GORGIAS *exits to* KNEMON's *house,* SOSTRATOS *to the shrine*]

[Choral Interlude]

ACT FIVE

[*Enter* SOSTRATOS *and* KALLIPPIDES *from the shrine*]

SOSTRATOS [*upset*]
You're not behaving, Father, in the way
I wanted. I expected more from you!   785

KALLIPPIDES
How's that? Didn't I consent? You *ought* to have
the girl you love! I'm willing.

SOSTRATOS [*reprovingly*]
                              Not completely.

KALLIPPIDES
By the gods, I am! I know that marriage
for youngsters is the most secure this way—
when it is entered into based on love.   790

SOSTRATOS
So I'm to marry Gorgias' sister, since
he's worthy of relationship with us.
But how then can you say you won't betroth
my sister to him in return?

KALLIPPIDES
                    That's bad?
[*Jokingly*] I'm not about to get two paupers in   795
the family at once! One's quite enough.

52

SOSTRATOS [*solemnly*]

You talk of money now. It comes and goes.
If you are sure it's going to always stay
with you, why go ahead—don't share a thing
you have with anyone. But if you're not   800
secure, and trust to luck for all you have,
you shouldn't be stingy with it, Father. Luck
will take away your cash and give it all
to someone else, perhaps to someone undeserving.
That's why I say you must yourself, as long   805
as you have money, use it generously,
Father. Be a help to all, and make
as many as you can lead better lives.
This is remembered always, even if
your luck should fail. Your friends will help you then.   810
A friend in sight is far more valuable
than hidden wealth, which you keep hoarded up.

KALLIPPIDES [*taken aback*]

You know me, Sostratos. I'm not about
to bury what I have with me. How could I?
It's yours. You think this man is worthy, and   815
you want him as a friend. All right. Good luck.
Why quote me proverbs? Go ahead, I'm willing.*
Be generous and share. I'm utterly
convinced by you.

SOSTRATOS

Convinced?

KALLIPPIDES

                        Yes, absolutely.
Don't let it worry you.

SOSTRATOS

                        I'll call him, then.   820

[*Enter* GORGIAS *from* KNEMON's *house*]

GORGIAS

I heard the whole of what you said
as I was coming out the door. Well . . .
I look upon you, Sostratos, as friendly,
and I am very fond of you myself.
But I don't want to get involved with things   825
too grand for me. I'm not cut out for them.

SOSTRATOS

What do you mean?

GORGIAS

I'm giving you my sister
as your wife. But as for marrying yours—
well, I'm reluctant.

SOSTRATOS

You're refusing?

GORGIAS

I don't believe a man should live on others' money.   830

SOSTRATOS

That's nonsense, Gorgias. You just don't think
you're worth enough to marry her.

GORGIAS

I think I'm worthy of her. But to take
a lot when I have little isn't right.

KALLIPPIDES*

By God, I think that while you're noble, you're   835
a trifle inconsistent.

GORGIAS

How?

KALLIPPIDES

You'd like to seem
content, although you're poor. Since I'm agreed,
why not give in?

GORGIAS

All right. I'd certainly be poor,
both in my wallet and my wits,
if I rejected my one chance to live.   840

SOSTRATOS

Well done!* Let's see to the betrothal now.

KALLIPPIDES [*to* GORGIAS]

My boy, I give to you my daughter for
your marriage, and to bear you children. And
as dowry, I bestow three talents.*

GORGIAS [*proudly*]

And I
have one to give as dowry for my sister.   845

KALLIPPIDES

Don't do too much, now.

GORGIAS

But I have the land.

KALLIPPIDES [*grandly*]

Keep all of it, my son. Now go and bring
your mother and your sister here to meet
the women in our clan.

GORGIAS [*bowled over*]
Oh, yes! Of course.

SOSTRATOS*

We'll stay here for the night, nearby the shrine,   850
and in the morning celebrate the weddings,
Gorgias. And bring along the old man
here. With us he'll be assured of getting
what he needs.

GORGIAS

He won't come willingly.

SOSTRATOS

Persuade him.

GORGIAS

If I can. [*Exit into* KNEMON's *house*]

SOSTRATOS

We ought to have   855
a fine drinking party now, Father,
and all-night vigils for the women.*

KALLIPPIDES [*ironically*]
They'll

be at the drinking, and it's we, I'm sure,
who'll watch all night. I'll go inside and get
things ready for you. [*Exit into the shrine*]

SOSTRATOS

Good idea. [*Exuberant*] A man   860
who's sensible should not despair of anything
at all. Hard work and care can get
you everything. Just now I've proof of this:
I've managed to arrange a match which no one
would have thought I could in just one day!   865
[*Enter* GORGIAS, *with his mother and sister*]

GORGIAS [*to the women*]

Let's go. A little faster.

SOSTRATOS [*seeing them*]
Over here!
[SOSTRATOS *leads them to the entrance to the shrine and calls to his mother inside*]
Receive these ladies, Mother!
[*They go in.* SOSTRATOS *turns back to* GORGIAS]
Knemon's not
come yet?

GORGIAS [*shaking his head*]
Why, he begged me to take away
old Simiche, so he would be alone
completely.

SOSTRATOS
What a man!

GORGIAS
Yes.

SOSTRATOS
Let him be.   870
We should go in.

GORGIAS [*hesitating*]
I'm pretty shy to be
with ladies, Sostratos . . .

SOSTRATOS
Oh, nonsense. Come!
You've got to think of them as "family" now.
[*Exeunt into the cave. Enter* SIMICHE *from* KNEMON's *house*]

SIMICHE
All right, all right, all right! I'll leave you too.
You'll lic there all alone. I pity you.   875
They wanted you to come, but you refused.
You're going to have a shock again, by God,
and it'll be worse than what you had just now.
[*Enter* GETA *from the shrine*]

GETA

I'll just come out and see . . .
[*He is interrupted by the noise of a flute, playing
at the party*]*
Why pipe at me, you wretched man? I can't enjoy it.   880
They've sent me out to check the invalid.
[*He shouts inside*]

Quit it!

[*The flute music stops momentarily, but is heard
throughout the following scene*]

SIMICHE [*addressing* GETA]

Let someone else go in and sit with him, I say.
I want to go and chat with mistress, say farewell
to her and hug her.

GETA

That's sensible. Go on inside.
Meanwhile I'll take care of him. [*Exit* SIMICHE]
[GETA *rubs his hands*] I've waited ages   885
for this chance, but couldn't leave my work in there . . .*
[*He peeps into* KNEMON's *house, and then walks over and
calls into the cave*]
. . . Sikon, come out here on the double! [*Turns back*]

Boy, we've got 889

some fun here!
[*Enter* SIKON *from the cave, a bit drunk*]

SIKON

You called?

GETA

I did indeed!   890
You want revenge for what you took back there?

SIKON [*indignant*]

I take it in the rear? Why don't you go and blow . . .*

GETA [*persisting, conspiratorially*]
The grouch is in there sleeping, all alone.

SIKON [*calming down and suddenly interested*]
                    And how's
he doing?

GETA
        Oh, not that bad.

SIKON [*catches his meaning, but is a bit hesitant*]
            He couldn't get up and hit us?

GETA [*ironically*]
I don't think he'll be doing any getting up.   895

SIKON
How sweet it is! I'll go in there and ask to borrow
something. He'll go berserk!

GETA [*suddenly*]
            Wait! You know what?
Why don't we first drag him out here and set him down,
and *then* start knocking on the door for favors? Oh,
we'll burn him! It will be fantastic!

SIKON
                I'm scared we might   900
be caught by Gorgias and beaten.

GETA
                No one will ever
hear us, with all the partying in there.
        [*Seriously*]   We surely
have to tame this reprobate. He's our relation
now, and he's a care to us. He'll be a burden
if he always acts like this.

SIKON [*cautiously*]
                              Just try to get him   905
out here without anyone seeing.

                    GETA [*gesturing toward the house*]
                              Go on, you first!

                    SIKON [*at the door, he turns*]
Wait just a minute, please! Don't go off and leave me!

                    GETA [*in a stage whisper*]
Shhh! Don't make a sound!

                    SIKON [*whispering back*]
                              I'm not making noise!
[*Together they exit into* KNEMON'S *house, and return in a
few seconds carrying the old man fast asleep on his bed*]*

                    GETA [*leading the way*]
To the right.

                    SIKON
          Okay.

                    GETA
               Right here.
[*They set down their burden*]
                              We're ready!

                    SIKON
                                   Fine!
I'll be the first. [*To the flutist inside*] Be sure
                    you keep time to my music!   910
[SIKON *starts beating on* KNEMON'S *door and shouting to
imaginary slaves inside*]
Slave! Little slave! Oh, fine slaves! Boy! Slaves!

KNEMON [*horrified, now that he is awake*]

I'm done for!

SIKON [*turns around to see* KNEMON, *feigns surprise*]

Hello! You live in here?

KNEMON [*angrily*]
Of course I do! What do you want?

SIKON

To borrow pots from you. I'd also like a bowl.

KNEMON [*furiously trying to stand up*]
Who'll help me up?

SIKON [*turns back to the door and shouts inside*]
I know you've got them—I just know it.   915
And also seven tripods and a dozen tables!
Be quick now, slaves! I'm in a hurry!

KNEMON
We haven't got them.

SIKON [*turning back to* KNEMON]
You haven't got them?

KNEMON
You heard me!

SIKON [*lightly*]
Oh! I'll run along then.

KNEMON [*moans*]
Oh, God! How miserable! How was I brought out here?
Who set me down in front here? [*Sees* GETA]
You get away from me!   920

GETA

All right.

[*He goes to the door of the house and starts pounding and shouting*]

Slave! Slave! Women! Men! Porter!

KNEMON

You madman, you're about to break the door!

GETA [*disregarding him*]
We need

nine mats from you!

KNEMON

From who?

GETA

And an Oriental

rug—a hundred-foot one!

KNEMON [*gnashing his teeth*]
Oh, I wish I had

my whip! [*Calling*] Simiche!!! Where is she?

GETA [*as before*]
Am I to go   925

to someone else for them?

KNEMON [*shouting*]
Oh! Stop!! SIMICHE!!!

[*He sees* SIKON, *who has walked over to him*]

May God take care you rot in hell! What do you want?

SIKON [*slowly and tormentingly*]

I'd like to have a large, bronze mixing bowl!

KNEMON [*purple with rage*]

Who'll help me up?

GETA [*comes over and, with* SIKON,
stands over the old man]
I'm sure you've got that Oriental, Pop—
I'm positive!

KNEMON
I haven't got it! Nor the bowl!   930
I'll kill that Simiche!

SIKON [*sternly*]
Sit still, and don't you grumble!
You're antisocial. You hate women. You won't come
to where we sacrifice. You'll have to bear all this, then.
There's no one here to help you. Go on and bite your
tongue . . .*   935
. . . Your wife and daughter first were welcomed with a
kiss   938
and now they're having a most pleasant time in there.
The party stories started. I prepared for the men's
drinking.   940
And also . . . [*He breaks off*]
Are you listening? Don't doze off!

GETA
No, indeed!

KNEMON [*groans*]
Ohhhh!

SIKON
So you wish you'd gone? I'll finish.
We offered wine. The couch was spread. I laid the tables—
for that's my job, you see —[*breaks off*]—you're listening, eh?
[*Portentously*]
Remember—I'm a master chef!

GETA [*believing he sees* KNEMON
weaken]
He's coming round.   945

SIKON [*continuing his description,
                and waxing eloquent*]
Another man decanted old and noble wine
into a vessel, mixing in a stream drawn from
the water of the Nymphs. He toasted all the men.
Another did it for the women. The drinking went on,
and on, and on.* You're listening? A tipsy girl, a maid,   950
who veiled her youthful face, stepped out to dance. The
                                                    flower
blushed as she began the rhythm. She trembled, shyly—
but another joined her hand in hers and waltzed!

GETA [*to* KNEMON]
You've been through hell. Now dance: come, get up on your
                                                    feet.

KNEMON
Whatever do you want, you wretches?

GETA
                            Come on, get up!   955
You're boorish.

KNEMON
            Damn it! No!

GETA
                Are we to take you in, then?

KNEMON [*desperately*]
What shall I do?

GETA [*picking up on his question*]
                Why, dance, of course!

KNEMON [*assenting wearily*]
                        Oh, take me, then.
Perhaps I'll bear things better inside.

GETA

That's wise. We win!*

Oh, victory! [*Calls for a slave into the shrine*]

Come, Donax! You, too, Sikon.

Lift this man up and take him in. [*To* KNEMON] And you   960
beware, because if we should catch you making
more trouble, we won't let you off as well
as we did this time.

[*Shouts into the shrine*] Ho! Bring out some crowns
for us, and bring a torch!

[*Hands* KNEMON *a garland*]

Here, take this.

That's fine.

[*He turns to the audience*]

Well, now, if you enjoyed our fight   965
with this old troublemaker, kindly give
us your applause—men, youths, and children: all!
May Victory, the noble maiden, friend
of laughter, stay our patron to the end!*

[*Donax and Sikon carry* KNEMON *into the shrine;*
GETA *follows*]

THE END

NOTES

102: bits of wood. Pyrrhias' phrase in the Greek is strange,
and there is much disagreement about what it means. The
word he uses for "wood" literally means a wooden instru-
ment of torture, placed like a yoke on the victim's neck so
that he is forced to stoop. Possibly Knemon's posture as
he prowls in the pear patch, and Pyrrhias' feeling that he
is some sort of monster, prompt the use of the word. But
possibly the word was used colloquially as a term of abuse,
and Pyrrhias breaks off for a moment to curse Knemon.

144: exit of Pyrrhias. I agree with Sandbach's argument that
this is the last we see of this character. Others hold that
he does not exit stage left (and thus back to town), but
rather to the cave, whence he reenters at 214 to console
Sostratos. The text at 214ff, however, is perfectly intelligible
with just Sostratos and Daos on stage; and a reappearance
by Pyrrhias would create a severe strain if, as seems likely,
Menander was restricted to three speaking actors who
shared all the roles in the play.

157: to stone. The "thing" that Perseus possessed is, of course,
the head of the gorgon Medusa. Sent by the evil king
Polydectes to kill Medusa, Perseus was aided in his mission
by Athena; he acquired some winged sandals, slew Medusa,
and returned to avenge himself by petrifying Polydectes.
As Sandbach notes, the extended reference to mythology is
an unusual and highly distinctive opening for Knemon. It
is the last thing we would expect from an enraged farmer,
and serves immediately to focus our interest on this
character "type."

188: Knemon's daughter. The list of *dramatis personae* in the papyrus does not assign Knemon's daughter a name, and both Sandbach and Handley believe that the Myrrhine referred to at line 709 (in a lacunose passage where sense is very difficult to restore) is Knemon's divorced wife, the mother of Gorgias. The wife is a nonspeaking character. No argument appears to me decisive here: whereas the name Myrrhine always belongs in New Comedy to an older, married woman, the authority of the list itself is reduced by its failure to include the mother of Sostratos, who probably speaks at 430. (But see the note on that passage.) I assign the daughter the name Myrrhine, and prefer to leave Gorgias' mother nameless, purely for dramatic convenience.

232: Choral Interlude. The nature of the choral performances in New Comedy cannot be determined. It is conjectured that the papyrus presents us with an abbreviation for the phrase "song of the chorus." But we have no idea what the song was, how it was related to the episodes of the play (if it was so related), whether it was accompanied by dancing, etc. Indeed, we are not even sure of the size of the chorus at this period, though some have inferred from a reference in Aristotle's *Politics* that the Aristophanic chorus of twenty-four had by the fourth century been reduced to fifteen. It seems likely that by Menander's time the choral interludes had little relation to the play's action and merely served as light entertainments between the acts. On the other hand, we should note how skillfully the chorus is introduced in Daos' concluding lines: similar motivation for the chorus's first appearance is found in three other Menandrian comedies.

247: the speech of Daos. The text is in bad condition here. We have lost the beginning of 247, in which Gorgias may have commanded Daos to knock at Knemon's door. An unusual amount of supplementation is necessary through verse 252, due to the bad condition of the papyrus.

301: I follow Handley's interpretation of Daos' remark here, and of Sostratos' reproof. The latter's abruptness seems better directed at Daos, who has interrupted him, than at Gorgias, whom he wishes to convince.

349: you can't win. The sentence after these words is guess-work, due to the state of the text. I follow Sandbach's reconstruction.

400: down the road. The Greek is more compressed than the English here, and is a fine example of Sikon's highly individual manner of speech. In one sentence he is made to combine two metaphors: he is being ground to mince-meat by the sheep, which is in turn compared to a large boat that is dragged along over land.

406: what . . . ? The text of this line is both mutilated and corrupt; the stage direction for Geta, his question, and Sikon's answer are all conjectural.

408: Paiania. Another district of Attica, about twenty miles from Phyle, where there was a shrine dedicated to Pan. The journey would be a considerable project.

430: Sostratos' mother. I follow Sandbach here in assigning a speaking part for Sostratos' mother, and in supposing that Sostratos' sister, mentioned at 794, is here identified by name.

471: debts. Athenians were accompanied by witnesses when they visited debtors and demanded payment: cf. Aristophanes, *Clouds* 1214ff.

522: Sostratos' speech. The situation of Sostratos is strikingly similar to that of Ferdinand in *The Tempest.* Both young men must undergo the trial of physical labor to prove their worth to their beloved's father. In Shakespeare, of course, Prospero directly imposes the trial on Ferdinand, and he regards his situation somewhat differently (cf. III.i.1ff).

549: chopping. The text is mutilated here: I follow Sandbach's interpretation and adopt with him the supplement of Arnott, *ta keramia,* in 549.

573: and respect you. Sostratos probably means to guard against leaving the impression of presumptuousness. He prophesies all on his own that everything will turn out all right; he then remembers the presence of Pan and hastens

to reassure the god of his devotion. At least, so I understand his afterthought. Sandbach believes that Sostratos
declares his *philanthropia* for Gorgias and Daos.

574: triple trouble's mine. The diction is as para-tragic in
Greek as in English. One may compare the punning salu-
tation to the dead at Aristophanes, *Frogs* 184.

585: dung in the yard. The Greek simply says "inside." It
would not, in fact, be surprising if Knemon and his
animals lived under the same roof.

597: forsaken now. Para-tragic self-pity: I follow Handley
and Winnington-Ingram on these lines. Sandbach objects
that it is inconsistent of Knemon to bewail his isolation; a
lonely life, after all, was what he chose. Yet inconsistency
is part of the characterization, and the humor is all the
greater in that this solemn reflection is prompted by the
loss of a mattock.

611: into the cave. I assume that Geta exits here in disgust
and does not wait to hear the ensuing dialogue.

622: drinks. The Greek here refers to libations, offerings to
the gods that were made at various points during a party.

634: a rabid dog inside a well. This appears to be a proverbial
expression. A fable of Aesop describes a gardener who
tries to rescue his dog from a well, only to be bitten by the
dog. I have added the word "rabid."

649: "Daddy!" The text is lacunose here, and restoration is
impossible.

689: Enter Knemon, Myrrhine, and Gorgias. How, precisely,
is Knemon brought out? Some believe that he is on a
rolling couch or chair: cf. the expression "wheel me in"
at 758. Sandbach argues that the *ekkyklema*, or rolling
machine, was used to reveal the interior of Knemon's
house. I am not entirely convinced. The most sensible
solution for production is to place Knemon on some sort
of rolling bed.

690: What a sight! Handley believes that Sostratos is referring
to Knemon here. But more consistent with his character is
an expression of admiration for Myrrhine (cf. 191–193,
above), and it is more amusing if he pays no attention to

Knemon: after all, he has just told us of his indifference to
the old man at 678ff.

702: standing there. Eight verses and part of a ninth are lost
here. Gorgias must be presumed to return with his mother
during the beginning of Knemon's great speech. It is
notable that with this speech the meter of the Greek
changes from iambic trimeter to trochaic tetrameter. I have
tried to reflect the change in the translation by employing
generally longer lines. Handley speculates that the change
of meter is intended "to underline the special nature of
the occasion"; it is true that this is the structural climax
of the play. The meter reverts to the standard iambic
trimeter at the beginning of the fifth act, but changes once
again, to iambic tetrameter, for the scene from 880 to 958.

755: wasting time all day. Two verses are lost here.

758: Exeunt Knemon and his family. Knemon must have
agreed to the marriage, or simply told Gorgias to arrange
things as he sees fit. I consider that the various supplements
offered for the two and one half verses between 758 and
760 are most uncertain, and so have left a gap until 761.

763: you deserve her. The text is corrupt here. I have translated the line as sense would seem to demand: cf.
Sandbach's note in *Commentary*, pp. 250–251.

817: I'm willing. A conjecture, since the last part of the line
is corrupt.

835: I adopt Sandbach's reconstruction for 836–840.

841: well done. I adopt the supplement of Barigazzi and Blake.

844: three talents. I have not substituted a modern equivalent,
since to do so would be artificial. The ancient evidence
suggests that Kallippides' offer is extremely generous;
wealthy families in Athens appear to have been satisfied
with far less.

850: I adopt Sandbach's suggestion for 850–851: cf. *Commentary*, p. 263.

857: all-night vigils for the women. Both men and women are
to be included in the party; Kallippides drags out an old
chestnut in the joke repertory of Greek comedy when he

suggests that the women will do more than their fair share of drinking.

880: Here the meter changes once again, to iambic tetrameter. The music of the flutist maintains the audience's awareness of the party inside the shrine, even as Knemon is being tormented on stage.

886: my work in there . . . Two lines (887–888) are lost here.

892: Sikon, drunk, misunderstands Geta's words (capable of a double meaning in Greek) and imposes a sexual sense on the question. He responds with a vulgar outburst, comparatively rare in New Comedy.

908: I infer that Knemon is carried out on his bed, though such is not mentioned.

935: bite your tongue. Two lines (936–937) are lost here. Sikon presumably begins his account of the party. His original objective, to spark envy and regret in Knemon, soon gives way to a lyrical, exuberant pleasure in the account for its own sake.

950: the drinking went on . . . The Greek here is uncertain. It is likely, however, that Sikon is more imaginative in the original than he is in translation: one possibility is that he conveys the soddenness of the occasion by comparing it to "watering a beach."

958: We win! This exclamation, and that of the following line (where the meter changes back to iambic trimeter), may also be related to Geta's explicit hope for the victory of Menander's play in the competition: see below on 969.

969: to the end. The request for applause, and for first prize in the dramatic competition, is a conventional element in New Comedy. The final couplet, whose formulaic quality I have tried to suggest by the rhyme in English, was used by Menander for the end of at least two other plays (cf. *Misoumenos* 465–466, *Sikyonios* 422–423).

BIBLIOGRAPHY

TEXTS

J.–M. Jacques, *Ménandre, Le Dyscolos* (Paris, 1963).
H. Lloyd–Jones, *Menandri Dyscolus* (Oxford, 1960).
F. H. Sandbach, *Menandri Reliquiae Selectae* (Oxford, 1972).

COMMENTARIES

E. W. Handley, *The Dyskolos of Menander* (Cambridge, Mass., 1965).
A. W. Gomme and F. H. Sandbach, *Menander, a Commentary* (Oxford, 1973).

CRITICISM

J. S. Feneron, "Some Elements of Menander's Style," *Bulletin of the Institute of Classical Studies* (London) 21 (1974) 81–95.
N. Holzberg, *Menander, Untersuchungen zur dramatischen Technik* (Nürnberg, 1974).
G. Meredith, *An Essay on Comedy*, in *Comedy*, ed. W. Sypher (Garden City, 1956).
F. H. Sandbach, "Menander's Manipulation of Language for Dramatic Purposes," in *Ménandre* (Entretiens Fondation Hardt 16, Geneva, 1970) 111–136.
E. Segal, "The *Physis* of Comedy," *Harvard Studies in Classical Philology* 77 (1973) 129–136.
T. B. L. Webster, *Studies in Menander*[2] (Manchester, 1960).
————, *An Introduction to Menander* (Manchester, 1974).